The
Old
Man's
Mitten

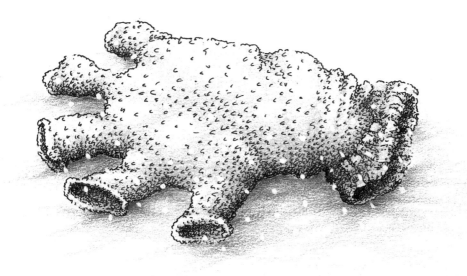

A Traditional Tale Retold by Yevonne Pollock   Illustrated by Trish Hill

This edition first published in the United States of America in 1994 by
MONDO Publishing

By arrangement with MULTIMEDIA INTERNATIONAL (UK) LTD

Printed in the United States of America
First Mondo printing, October 1994
00 01   9 8 7 6

Originally published in Australia in 1986 by Horwitz Publications Pty Ltd
Original development by Robert Andersen & Associates and Snowball Educational

Library of Congress Cataloging-in-Publication Data
Pollock, Yevonne.
    The old man's mitten : a Ukrainian tale / retold by Yevonne Pollock ;
illustrated by Trish Hill.
        p.   cm.
    Summary: A mouse, a frog, a rabbit, a fox, a wolf, and a bear all squeeze into
a lost mitten until its owner comes back to reclaim it.
    ISBN 1-879531-69-0 : $21.95. — ISBN 1-879531-60-7 : $4.95
    [1. Folklore—Ukraine. 2. Mittens—Folklore. 3. Animals—Folklore] I. Hill,
Trish, ill. II. Title.
PZ8.1.P858401   1994
398.2'0947'710452—dc20
[E]   94-30195
                                                                  CIP
                                                                  AC

ONCE UPON A TIME an old man went
for a walk in the woods with his dog.
He dropped one of his mittens in the
snow as he went on his way.

Along came Munch-crunch Mouse.

She looked inside the mitten.
She hopped inside the mitten.
It was warm and soft.
"This is where I'll live," she squeaked.

So Munch-crunch Mouse curled up
inside.

Then came Hop-stop Frog.
He looked inside the mitten.
He hopped inside the mitten.

It was warm and soft.
"This is where I'll live," he croaked.

So Hop-stop Frog and Munch-crunch
Mouse curled up inside.

Next came Fleet-feet Rabbit.
She looked inside the mitten.
She hopped inside the mitten.
It was warm and soft.
"This is where I'll live," she snuffled.

So Fleet-feet Rabbit, Hop-stop Frog,
and Munch-crunch Mouse curled up
inside. They were just right!

Soon came Smiley-wiley Fox.
He looked inside the mitten.
He hopped inside the mitten.
It was warm and soft.
"This is where I'll live," he yapped.

So Smiley-wiley Fox, Fleet-feet Rabbit,
Hop-stop Frog, and Munch-crunch
Mouse curled up inside. They were
getting rather crowded!

Later came Howly-prowly Wolf.
She looked inside the mitten.
She hopped inside the mitten.
It was warm and soft.
"This is where I'll live," she growled.

So Howly-prowly Wolf, Smiley-wiley Fox,
Fleet-feet Rabbit, Hop-stop Frog, and
Munch-crunch Mouse curled up inside.
They were getting *very* crowded!

At last came
Grumbly-rumbly Bear.
He looked inside the mitten.
He hopped inside the mitten.
It was warm and soft.
"This is where I'll live," he roared.

So Grumbly-rumbly Bear, Howly-prowly
Wolf, Smiley-wiley Fox, Fleet-feet Rabbit,
Hop-stop Frog, and Munch-crunch
Mouse curled up inside. They were
EXTREMELY crowded!

Just then they heard the old man's dog.
"WOOF! WOOF!" it barked.

Out of the mitten
tumbled Grumbly-rumbly Bear,
Howly-prowly Wolf, Smiley-wiley Fox,
Fleet-feet Rabbit, Hop-stop Frog, and
Munch-crunch Mouse.

"Let's go," roared Grumbly-rumbly Bear.
"I'm off," growled Howly-prowly Wolf.
"Goodbye," yapped Smiley-wiley Fox.
"See you later," snuffled Fleet-feet Rabbit.
"I'm going too," croaked Hop-stop Frog.
"Oh dear," squeaked Munch-crunch
Mouse. "It was so warm and soft."

They all ran off into the woods.

Along came the old man and his dog.

The man picked up his mitten and
went on his way and that was the
end of that.